Laura Campbell is a mother of two who knows the importance of a good bedtime story. Working in the insurance industry by day, Laura leads a very ordinary life but has never lost her passion for a good fairy story. So when her children were born she wanted to give them the same experience of a great story so that they always ended the day with a happy thought. Laura is now realising a dream she has always had of putting her stories into publication and proving that no matter what path you take in life and no matter how long it takes you, your dreams are always achievable.

THE RAINBOW

Leaves A Trail

Laura Campbell

AUSTIN MACAULEY PUBLISHERS™

LONDON ★ CAMBRIDGE ★ NEW YORK ★ SHARJAH

A CIP catalogue record for this title is available from the British Library.

ISBN 9781398432444 (Paperback)
ISBN 9781398432451 (ePub e-book)

www.austinmacauley.com

First Published 2022
Austin Macauley Publishers Ltd®
1 Canada Square
Canary Wharf
London
E14 5AA

I would like to thank my amazing mum and dad – two ordinary people who taught me to believe I was extraordinary and always encouraged me to follow my dreams.

Itzy was a very busy fairy who lived in Willow Wind Woods. She lived behind one of the fairy doors created by all the good boys and girls of the village. Each fairy gets to choose their home when a new fairy door is added. As soon as Itzy saw her new home, she knew straightaway that it was made for her as it had a beautiful bright rainbow painted on it. This was perfect for Itzy as her job in the fairy kingdom was this: after every rainstorm she had to prepare all her bright and colourful paints and paint the bright and beautiful rainbow to lighten up the dull, grey sky.

Her best friend was Bitzy the fairy who had to be ready with the magic penny for the very lucky boy or girl who found it and got to make a wish. As you may know, you can find the gold coin right at the place where the rainbow touches the ground. That very day there was the most enormous thunder and rain. Well, it almost felt like it would never stop pouring down. Itzy and Bitzy were so frightened that they spent the whole time hiding under their tiny beds.

At last the rain finally stopped and Itzy added some fairy dust to make her rainbow extra bright to lighten up the dull grey sky.

When she was done, Bitzy placed the magic penny under a fallen leaf, right at the spot where the rainbow touched the ground.

The two fairies were very cold so after their job was done, they flew home as quick as they could for a nice cup of hot coco.

While they were drinking their coco, they heard a very loud knock on their door. When Itzy opened it, there standing in front of them was Gizzy, the very naughty gnome.

"What do you want, Gizzy? I hope you are not here to cause us any trouble?"
"Oh no, I was just admiring your beautiful rainbow, Itzy, and I wanted to ask you for a teeny, tiny favour?"
"And what's that?" asked Itzy.

"Well, I was just wondering if you would let me help paint one of the colours the next time you're painting the rainbow, pretty please?"

"Certainly not! I told you the last time, when you spilled all of my lovely paints and made my beautiful rainbow a horrible mess, that you were never touching any of my paints ever again!"
"I know, but I promise to be careful this time, pleeease?" begged Gizzy.

"No! and that is my final answer, Gizzy. Now goodbye!" said Itzy.

And with that, Itzy slammed the door closed in his face and went back to drinking her coco.

In a big sulk, Gizzy made his way back home, all the time thinking of a plan of revenge to get back at Itzy for being so mean to him. Then a most mischievous plan came to him. He was going to steal Itzy's paints. If he couldn't paint the rainbow, then neither could she, or anyone else for that matter.

That very night while Itzy and Bitzy were fast asleep in their beds made from the softest lily petals, Gizzy crept inside through the window, and the naughty gnome stole all Itzy's paints from her paint box.

He then very quietly crept back out of the window, taking each paint pot one at a time, so as not to wake the very sleepy fairies who were still fast asleep in their beds.

However, as he took the last paint pot through the window, he didn't notice that he had accidently knocked the lid off, leaving drops of paint from the window pane all the way home and into his shed, where he hid them at the bottom of his garden.

The next morning when Itzy woke up, she was shocked and upset to see that all her lovely paints were gone.

She started to cry bitterly but Bitzy, who was angry that someone would steal in the fairy kingdom, told Itzy to dry her tears and that they will report straight to the king fairy.

He would be most angry to learn that a very naughty fairy in his kingdom was a thief.

As Itzy and Bitzy left the house to make their way to the king, they noticed a trail of red paint and knew straightaway that it had come from Itzy's paints. They changed their plan and decided to follow the trail, and that would surely lead them straight to the thief. They followed the trail all the way to Gizzy's shed where the trail stopped.

"I knew it!" exclaimed Itzy. "I knew it was that naughty gnome! Just because I wouldn't let him paint the rainbow. I shall go in there right now and give him a good telling off!"

"No! Wait, Itzy. Don't you see if we wait until he goes into the shed, we can catch him red-handed? And then we will go straight to the king and tell him."

Itzy agreed and the two fairies waited patiently behind the gate in the garden, peeking through the gap to watch for Gizzy coming out of his house.

Sure enough, Gizzy came out and went straight into the shed and as he opened it, the two fairies could see all of Itzy's paints on the top shelf inside the shed.
Itzy and Bitzy then ran from behind the gate and towards Gizzy. They pushed the naughty gnome inside the shed and closed the door behind him. They locked it up and went to the king, and after telling him what Gizzy had done, the king was so mad that he went along with Itzy and Bitzy back to Gizzy's shed to see for himself what Gizzy had done.

As they opened the door to the shed, there was Gizzy standing with red hands from the red paint that had dripped all over him.

"He really has been caught red-handed now," said Itzy laughing.

The king punished the now-very-sorry gnome by giving him the job of cleaning all of Itzy's brushes after she had painted the rainbow, until he proved that he could behave like all the magical creatures in Willow Wind Woods.

As for Itzy and Bitzy, well if you look very closely after the rain, then you might just see the two tiny fairies busy doing their job of brightening up the sky with a lovely rainbow. Remember though, that only the very good boys and girls will find the magic penny. If you have a fairy trail near you, be sure to paint a bright and beautiful fairy door as with a touch of magic from their wands, you will be giving a new fairy a home.

THE END